BRIGHT and EARLY Books
for BEGINNING Beginners

GROLIER
BOOK CLUB EDITION

Hooper Humperdink...?

NOT HIM!

Hooper Humperdink...? NOT HIM!

By Theo. LeSieg

Illustrated by Charles E. Martin

A Bright & Early Book
From BEGINNER BOOKS
A Division of Random House, Inc., New York

L M N O

I'm going to have a party.
But I don't think
that I'll ask

Hooper Humperdink.

I'll ask Alice.

I'll ask Abe.

I'll ask Bob
and Bill
and Babe.

I'll ask Charlie, Clara, Cora.
Danny, Davey, Daisy, Dora.

I'll ask Dinny. I'll ask Dot.

But Hooper Humperdink . . . ?
I'LL NOT!

Elma! Elly! Ethel! Ed!
Frieda, Francis, Frank and Fred.

I'll ask George and Gus and Gary.
Henry, Hedda, Hank and Harry!

I'll ask every kid I like.
Irene, Ivy, Izzy, Ike.
Joe and Jerry, Jack and Jim.

But Hooper Humperdink . . . ?
NOT <u>HIM</u>!

That Humperdink!
I don't know why,
but somehow
I don't like that guy.

A party needs
a band to play.

And so I'll get a band.
O.K.

The K. K. Kats
are on their way!

And I like
Lucy, Luke and Lum.
I like the Lesters.
They can come.

And Mark and Mary!
Mike and Mabel!
I'll have to get
a bigger table!

They'll come by air,
by parachute.

Nora,
Norton,
Nat
and Newt!

And Olivetta Oppenbeem!
I'll have to order more ice cream!

I'll need about ten tons,
I think.

But <u>none</u> for
Hooper Humperdink!

No! Humperdink won't do at all.
He's not good fun
like Pete and Paul,
and Pinky, Pat and Pasternack.
I bet they come by camel back.

And so will
lots of other pals,
like the Perkins boys
and the Plimton gals!

Q . . . Q . . . Q . . .
Who begins with "Q"?
Quintuplets!

So I'll ask a few.

Ralph and Rudolf!
Ruth and Russ!

And some other R's
in a big blue bus.

Oh, what a party!
Sally! Sue!
Solly! Sonny!
Steve and Stoo!

I'll ask the Simpson sisters, too.

But
I'm not asking
<u>YOU</u> <u>KNOW</u> <u>WHO</u>!

Nobody
wants to play with Hooper.
Humperdink's a party-pooper!

Welcome, Tim and Tom and Ted!
Grab a hot dog. Get well fed.

Welcome, Ursula! Welcome, Ubb!
Strawberry soda by the tub!

Welcome, Vera!
Violet! Vinny!
Welcome, Wilbur, Waldo, Winnie!

Xavier!
And Yancy! Yipper!
Zacharias!
Zeke and Zipper!

All my good friends from A to Z!
The biggest gang you'll ever see!
The biggest gang there'll ever be!

A party big and good as this
is too good for <u>anyone</u> to miss!

And so, you know, I sort of think . . .

. . . I <u>WILL</u> ask
Hooper Humperdink!

By Theo. LeSieg

. . . readily admits to being heavily influenced in his style by the great Dr. Seuss. In fact, the main difference between them is that while Dr. Seuss is an artist of remarkable capabilities, Theo. LeSieg can't draw a lick. He is a marvelous writer, though, and ever since he was discovered on a mountaintop in California by Dr. Seuss (where coincidentally, Dr. Seuss also lives), he has been writing delightful books for children.

Charles E. Martin

. . . may be more familiar as C.E.M., the artist who does the marvelous cover paintings for *The New Yorker*. His witty cartoons also appear under those initials in many magazines and newspapers. Mr. Martin's paintings and drawings have been exhibited widely, and his work is represented in several museums, including the Museum of the City of New York. Mr. and Mrs. Martin live in New York City and also have a home on lovely Monhegan Island, Maine. The Martins have one son, a busy actor, and a grandson.